RACCOON!

RACCOON!

By E.Q. Wright

For Olivia Rose

www.EQwright.com

Text & interior illustrations copyright © 2018 by E.Q. Wright

CreateSpace Independent Publishing Platform, North Charleston, SC

ISBN: 1722330716
ISBN-13: 978-1722330712

3 5 7 9 10 8 6 4 2

"Raccoon! Raccoon!"

A girl shouted and pointed up.

The raccoon looked down,
but didn't budge.

Others heard the girl and looked up.

"RACCOON! RACCOON!" They all shouted together.

Still, the raccoon didn't move.

"Let's help it down," a man said.

But just as they tried, the raccoon began to climb UP.
Everyone's eyes opened wide.

"RACCOON! RACCOON!"

They all shouted again.

The raccoon didn't look down this time.

She just kept climbing higher.

And higher.

And higher still.

She climbed for such a long time, that night had arrived.

The raccoon was very tired,
and slept upon a window ledge under the moonlight.

She awoke the next morning and looked down.

Her eyes opened wide.

No raccoon had ever been this high before.

"RACCOON!

RACCOON!"

If she reached the roof, someone could help her.
So instead of shouting to climb down,
everyone cheered, "Keep climbing! Don't give up!"

She looked towards the sky, and kept going.

"Raccoon! Raccoon!"

"Raccoon! Raccoon!"

"Hayawan alrrakun! Hayawan alrrakun!"

"Ek prakaar ka jaanavar! Ek prakaar ka jaanavar!"

People began talking about the raccoon around the world.

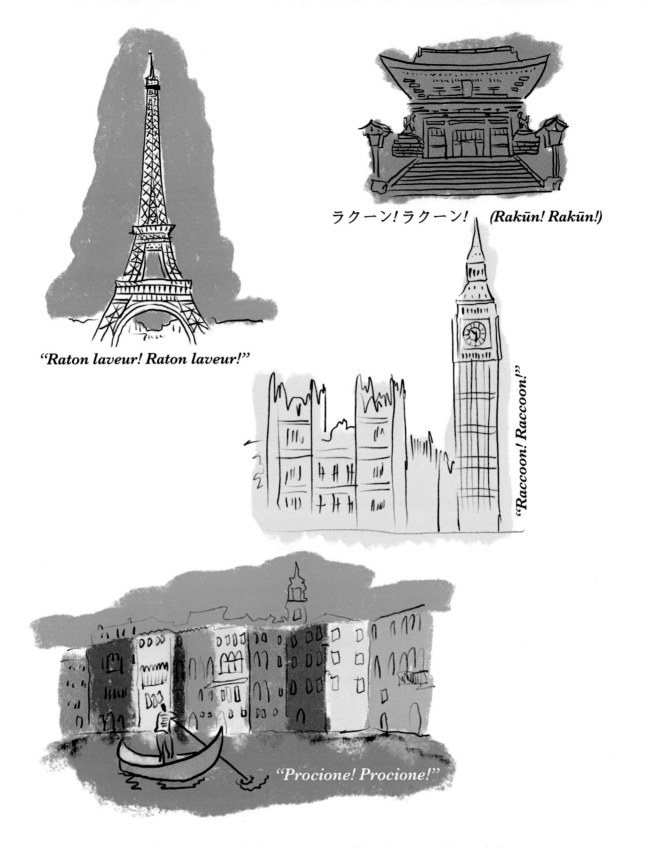

"Raton laveur! Raton laveur!"

ラクーン! ラクーン!　*(Rakūn! Rakūn!)*

"Raccoon! Raccoon!"

"Procione! Procione!"

"Raccoon! Raccoon!" they all said,
and hoped for a happy ending.

She was hungry and thirsty.

But she was also strong and brave.

As she climbed up higher, it became windy.

She held on tight, and didn't give up.

After what felt like forever,

she reached the top of the building.

"RACCOON!

RACCOON!"

The world cheered.

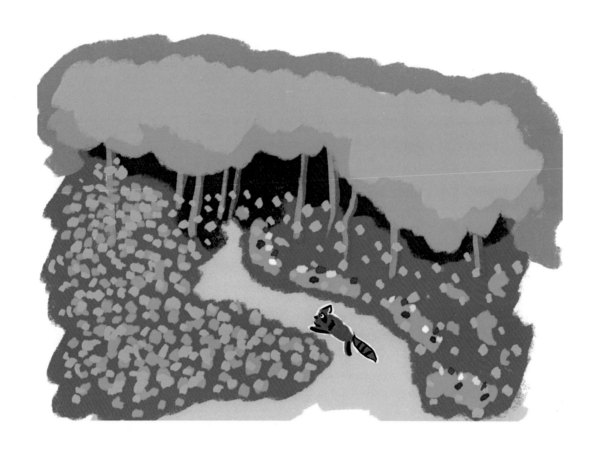

Later that day she was brought to the woods,
sprinted towards the trees, and lived happily ever after.

Author & illustrator E.Q. Wright
is an Education Intern
at Como Park Zoo & Conservatory.
He lives with his wife and daughter
in Saint Paul, MN
(the same neighborhood as the
raccoon who dared to climb).

www.EQwright.com

Made in the USA
Lexington, KY
07 October 2018